PARK SCHOOL

Birthday Book
Club

Donated in Honor of:

Alison Parisea

Donated on: 3/10/95

ELVIRA

by MARGARET SHANNON

TICKNOR & FIELDS / *Books for Young Readers* / New York • 1993

Copyright © 1991 by Margaret Shannon
First American edition 1993 published by Ticknor & Fields,
A Houghton Mifflin company, 215 Park Avenue South,
New York, New York 10003.
First published in Australia by Omnibus Books

Manufactured in the United States of America
The text of this book is set in 18 pt. ITC Zapf International Medium.
The illustrations are pen and ink with watercolor, reproduced in full color.
HOR 10 9 8 7 6 5 4 3 2 1

Library of Congress Cataloging-in-Publication Data

Shannon, Margaret.
Elvira / text and illustrations by Margaret Shannon. — 1st
American ed.
p. cm.
Summary: A young dragon who prefers making daisy chains and
dressing up to fighting and eating princesses finds a way
to be who she is.
ISBN 0-395-66597-3
[1. Dragons—Fiction. 2. Identity—Fiction.] I. Title.
PZ7.S52884E1 1993
[E]—dc20   92-39784   CIP   AC

To my mother

HUNDREDS OF YEARS AGO, there was a group
of the meanest, nastiest dragons that ever lived.

They liked nothing better than fighting other dragons
and gobbling up princesses.

When Elvira was born she seemed just like
any other baby dragon.

But soon her mother and father noticed
that she wasn't quite like the others.
She didn't like eating princesses…

and she didn't like fighting.

What Elvira liked was sitting on the grass making daisy chains.

The other little dragons teased her
and burned her daisy chains.

This made Elvira angry.

But it didn't change her. She began making dresses,
and spent hours admiring herself.

The others teased her even more.

This made Elvira furious.

"Well, dear, if you would only behave like
a *normal* dragon—" her mother said.

"You want me to be like *them*?"
This was too much.

So, she packed her dresses in a suitcase and went to live where dresses and daisy chains were appreciated.

At first the princesses were not happy to see her,

but once they were sure she was not going to eat them,
she became their favorite pet. They dressed her in pretty clothes,
polished her scales, and curled her eyelashes.

They even painted her claws. Elvira was thrilled.

One day, when Elvira was sitting in the forest,
she saw her mother and father coming toward her.

"Hello! Hello!" she cried. They stopped and stared.

"This is the biggest, fattest princess I have ever seen!"
said her father. And he grabbed her with his big claw,
ready to swallow her whole.

"Dad, it's me!" Elvira screamed.
And she proved it.

Elvira's parents were glad to see her.

"It's time for you to come home, Elvira," her mother said.

"You don't want to be mistaken for a princess again."

The other little dragons heard that Elvira was back,
and went to welcome her.

When they saw her, they gasped.

Elvira's clothes were beautiful.

(The princesses had taught her a thing or two.)

Soon all the dragons wanted dresses like Elvira's.

She made dozens of them.

Everyone was happy...

except, of course,

the princesses.

E
S   Shannon, Margaret
           Elvira

$13.45

DATE			

Primary